NO STRANGERS

Sharrie Warner

Illustrator Hinesman Dukes

Book Designer: s . a . m .

To order additional copies of this book, contact:
Xlibris Corporation
1-888-795-4274
www.Xlibris.com
Orders@Xlibris.com

Mom and Dad,
"Why can't I talk to
STRANGERS

STRANGERS
are people we
don't know.

Always remember never leave your parent's sight! Stay Visible! Scream or Yell, if a STRANGER tries to do anything to you!

Here are some
examples that identify
who a STRANGER is...
LISTEN AND LEARN

A STRANGER
is someone walking pass
on the street or someone
standing in line at the
grocery store.

A STRANGER is someone who is sitting in a parked car on any street.

A STRANGER may ask for help finding a lost dog or item.

A STRANGER is someone who tries to give or offer you something without your parent's permission.

A STRANGER may offer you a ride home. A stranger may try to give you a toy or some candy.

A STRANGER may persuade you to get in the car with them.

A STRANGER is someone who is sitting across from your school or from the park...

These are Red Flags!
STOP!

These signs will let you know that the person is a STRANGER..............

Always get permission
first from someone you know
before speaking to
STRANGERS.

Ask your parent
or teacher for
Permission.

A STRANGER
may look just like you...

Thanks,
Mom and Dad...

I won't
talk to any
strangers.

Shhhh...

LISTEN,

BE ALERT,
BE SAFE
AND
BE SMART!

All Children

This story was written for all
children and children with autism who
has to visualize things in order to
process the information in their minds.

Thank You **Sharon Rogers** for the
Vision of Autism